WALT DISNEY PICTURES'

OLIVER & Company

Oliver Finds a Home

By Justine Korman
Illustrated by Al White Studios

A GOLDEN BOOK • NEW YORK
Western Publishing Company, Inc., Racine, Wisconsin 53404

Dodger was a cool, streetwise dog. He hummed a jazzy
tune as he strutted up and down the avenues of New York.
This was his town. He loved the sounds and sights of
the streets.

Dodger laughed when he saw Louie, the sausage vendor, struggling to fend off a homeless and hungry kitten.

"Hey! Get off me!" Louie exclaimed, and he threw the kitten onto a pile of trash.

"Pssst, kitty!" Dodger hissed.

The cat looked fearfully at Dodger from under a banana peel.

"Chill out! I don't eat cats—too much fur," the big dog said. "Besides, if we team up, those sausages are ours. All you need is a plan with some street smarts."

The kitten, Oliver, listened while Dodger explained his plan. Oliver was a bit doubtful, but smelling those sausages made him ready to try anything.

So Dodger chased Oliver up Louie's shirt. While Louie struggled to remove the clawing kitten, Dodger ran off with the sausages.

"We did it!" Oliver exclaimed when he caught up with Dodger.

"You were great, kid. But I've got to go," said the dog.

"What about my share?" Oliver protested. Dodger shrugged and strutted away.

"That's not fair!" Oliver complained, hurrying to keep up.

"Fairs are for tourists!" Dodger shouted, breaking into a fast run. "Consider this a free lesson in street smarts from New York's coolest canine!" Dodger tried to run away from Oliver, but the kitten followed him.

Dodger was surprised at how well Oliver kept up with him, running through traffic, under sawhorses, and even across the top of a cement mixer. Oliver kept following, despite being splashed with cement and blasted by water from a fire hydrant.

Then Dodger hopped aboard a piano being hauled up to a window in a nearby apartment. Oliver tried to jump on the piano, too, but his leap sent him sailing clear over the other side of it. He landed with a splat on a pyramid of tomatoes at a vegetable stand.

"So much for kitty," Dodger concluded. "Time to head home to the gang."

As Dodger approached a beat-up barge that belonged to a man named Fagin, he heard the other members of the gang talking. They were hungry and were arguing over who was supposed to have brought home supper.

"It was your turn, Frankie," whined Tito, the Chihuahua.

"My name is Francis, not Frankie," the bulldog replied in a lofty voice.

"Man, your name will be mud when Fagin gets here and there's nothing—" Tito stopped in mid-sentence as the chain of sausages landed at his feet.

"New York's coolest canine comes through again," Dodger declared. "But not without a struggle."

"You're the greatest, man!" said Tito.

"You are our major benefactor," Francis proclaimed.

"Yeah...and you're OK, too!" stammered big, dumb, but lovable Einstein.

"How did you do it this time, Dodgie baby?" asked Rita, the almost-Afghan, full of admiration.

"Was there a fight? How many were there?" Tito demanded.

Dodger held up a paw, then began after a dramatic pause.

"There was this monster...a greedy, ugly, crazy monster with razor-sharp claws and dripping fangs. He came at me, eyes burning. Suddenly..."

Suddenly, with a bang and a screech and a terrible crash, part of the roof of the barge collapsed. All the dogs ran for cover, even the daring Dodger.

When the dust settled, the dogs peeked out from their hiding places.

"What was that?" Rita asked. But no one knew.

Tito circled the pile of wreckage, and something moved. He sniffed.

Then Oliver emerged, and Rita giggled. Oliver proceeded to tell the gang what had really happened with the sausages.

"You're awfully cute for a monster," Rita said.

The dogs had a good laugh at Dodger's expense, and a free-for-all followed. Oliver took cover in the cardboard box where the dogs put the things they brought home each day.

Just then Fagin came home. "What's going on?" he cried. "Sykes will be here any minute!"

The fight stopped instantly, and the dogs rushed to greet Fagin, licking his face and wagging their tails.

Fagin grabbed the cardboard box to see what his dogs had collected. There was an empty wallet, a broken tennis racket, and...a cat?

"Heh-heh! Hi, kitty!" said Fagin. "You're pretty cute." Then he sighed.

"But cute isn't enough for Sykes." Sykes was an evil man who took everything Fagin and his dogs could find.

A car horn blared outside. Sykes had arrived! While Fagin pleaded with Sykes, Sykes's dogs boarded the barge to make trouble of their own.

Sykes's two Dobermans, Roscoe and DeSoto, prowled
the barge. While Roscoe insulted Tito and Einstein,
DeSoto followed his nose to Oliver's hiding place. Sykes's
horn honked outside, but DeSoto only moved closer to
Oliver. He bared all his teeth in a terrible grin.

"I like cats," DeSoto growled. "I like them for supper!"

Just as the dog was about to bite, Oliver reached up and clawed his nose.

"Yeow!" DeSoto shrieked, reeling backward.

Roscoe rushed to his defense, and the two furious Dobermans glared at Oliver and showed their razor-sharp fangs. Oliver saw all of his nine lives flash before his eyes.

In the nick of time Dodger sprang up to help Oliver,
stepping between the Dobermans and the frightened
kitten. But then Sykes's horn blared outside again.

"Run along, boys. Your master's calling," Rita taunted.

"We'll get you next time, Dodger," Roscoe snarled.
"And your cat, too!"

When the Dobermans were gone, Dodger winked
at Oliver.

Then Fagin shuffled gloomily back to the barge.

"Sykes wants some more stuff soon, or I'm in trouble," Fagin said.

The dogs did their best to cheer him up. Dodger brought Fagin's footstool, and Tito brought Fagin's slippers. Rita and Francis pulled a blanket over him, and Einstein gave Fagin a dog biscuit he'd been saving.

"Thanks, guys," Fagin said. "We'll make it somehow."
And a shadow of a smile crossed his lips when he saw all
the eager faces looking at him.

"I saw DeSoto's nose," Fagin said. "Which one of you
did that?"

Dodger pushed Oliver toward Fagin's chair.

"You? You little— Why, that took courage!" Fagin
stammered, and he broke into a wide smile.

"We've never had a cat in the gang before," Fagin began. "But we can use all the help we can get."

So Oliver became a member of Fagin's gang. They all shared the sausages, and then Fagin read them a bedtime story.

The gang settled down to sleep on blankets and boxes
scattered all over Fagin's barge. Oliver curled up next to
Dodger. He felt warm and safe, and he started to purr.

Just before he fell asleep, Oliver looked around him and
said with a sigh, "These are my friends. This is my home."